KU-344-589

Usborne Farmyard Tales

BARN ON FIRE

Heather Amery

Illustrated by Stephen Cartwright

Language Consultant: Betty Root
Reading and Language Information Centre
University of Reading, England

There is a little yellow duck to find on every page.

This is Apple Tree Farm

Mrs Boot is the farmer. She has two children
called Poppy and Sam, and a dog called Rusty.

This is Ted.

Ted works at Apple Tree Farm. He looks after the tractor and all the other farm machines.

Poppy and Sam help Ted.

They like helping Ted with jobs on the farm.
Today he is mending the fence round the sheep field.

4

Sam smells smoke.

"Ted," says Sam, "I think something's burning."
Ted stops working and they all sniff hard.

The barn is on fire.

"Look," says Poppy, "there's smoke coming from the hay barn. It must be on fire. What shall we do?"

"Call the fire brigade."

"Come on," says Ted. "Run to the house and tell your Mum to call the fire brigade. Run as fast as you can."

Poppy and Sam run to the house.

"Mum, Mum," shouts Poppy. "Call the fire brigade."
"The hay barn is on fire. Quickly, Mum."

Mrs Boot dials the number.

"It's Apple Tree Farm." she says. "The fire brigade, please, as fast as you can. Thank you very much."

"You must stay here."

"Now, Poppy," says Mrs Boot. "I want you and Sam to stay indoors. And don't let Rusty out."

Poppy and Sam watch from the door.

Soon they hear the siren. Then the fire engine roars up the road and into the farmyard.

"The firemen are here."

The firemen jump down from the engine. They lift down lots of hoses and unroll them.

12

The firemen run toward the barn with the hoses.
Can you see where they get the water from?

13

The firemen squirt water on to the barn.

Poppy and Sam watch them from the window.
"It's still burning on the other side," says Poppy.

"There's the fire."

One fireman runs round the barn. What a surprise!
Two campers are cooking on a big wood fire.

The fire is out.

"We're sorry," say the campers. "It was exciting," says Sam, "but I'm glad the barn is all right."

First published in 1989. Usborne Publishing Ltd, 20 Garrick Street, London WC2E 9BJ, England. © Usborne Publishing Ltd. 1989.

The name Usborne and the device are Trade Marks of Usborne Publishing Ltd. All rights reserved. No part of this publication may be reproduced, stored in a retrieval system or transmitted by any form or by any means, electronic, mechanical photocopy, recording or otherwise, without the prior permission of the publisher. Printed in Portugal.